Agatha

Girl of Mystery

GROSSET & DUNLAP
Published by the Penguin Group
Penguin Group (USA) LLC, 375 Hudson Street, New York, New York 10014, USA

USA | Canada | UK | Ireland | Australia | New Zealand | India | South Africa | China

penguin.com
A Penguin Random House Company

Original Title: Agatha Mistery: Il tesoro delle Bermuda
Text by Sir Steve Stevenson
Original cover and illustrations by Stefano Turconi

English language edition copyright © 2014 Penguin Group (USA) LLC. Original edition published by Istituto Geografico De Agostini S.p.A., Italy © 2011 Atlantyca Dreamfarm s.r.l., Italy

International Rights © Atlantyca S.p.A.—via Leopardi 8, 2013 Milano, Italia
foreignrights@atlantyca.it-www.atlantyca.com

Published in 2014 by Grosset & Dunlap, a division of Penguin Young Readers Group, 345 Hudson Street, New York, New York 10014. GROSSET & DUNLAP is a trademark of Penguin Group (USA) LLC. Printed in the USA.

Library of Congress Cataloging-in-Publication Data is available.

ISBN 978-0-448-46224-0

10 9 8 7 6 5 4 3 2 1

Agatha
Girl of Mystery

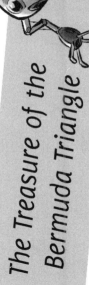

The Treasure of the
Bermuda Triangle

by Sir Steve Stevenson
illustrated by Stefano Turconi

translated by Siobhan Tracey
adapted by Maya Gold

Grosset & Dunlap
An Imprint of Penguin Group (USA) LLC

SIXTH MISSION

Agents

Agatha
Twelve years old, an aspiring mystery writer; has a formidable memory

Dash
Agatha's cousin and student at the private school Eye International Detective Academy

Chandler
Butler and former boxer with impeccable British style

Watson
Obnoxious Siberian cat with the nose of a bloodhound

Uncle Conrad
Energetic, tanned, and athletic; a water-park owner and dolphin lover

DESTINATION

The island of Bermuda

Bermuda

OBJECTIVE

Learn the true story of how a priceless gold Mayan calendar disappeared in the infamous Bermuda Triangle

The Investigation Begins . . .

It was a blustery Saturday morning in late January, and Dashiell Mistery, an aspiring detective at the prestigious Eye International Detective Academy, was jumping out of his skin with excitement. He had just received an Evite from his friend Mallory, inviting him to her birthday party.

Dash was thrilled. He'd dragged himself out of bed to sit through an online seminar on Espionage and Counterespionage, and had been struggling to cover his yawns for two hours when Mallory's message popped up on his screen. He managed to prop his eyes open till noon, said a polite good-bye to Professor DM31, and immediately opened Mallory's invitation.

Her party would start at eight o'clock at Fashionista, an exclusive club in the center of London. The theme was the seventies, and guests were invited to "dress disco" in honor of that era's most popular music. The Evite was covered with vintage graphics of people wearing bell-bottom pants, multicolored shirts with pointed collars, suffocatingly tight vests, and platform shoes with chunky, wedged heels.

Dash loved costumes and disguises, and he decided to pull out all the stops. He was starving, so he wolfed down a take-out container of fries that had been in the fridge for at least three days. Then he started rummaging through his closet, but all he could find were jeans, T-shirts, and a couple of sweaters and suits his mother had bought him for special occasions.

The Investigation Begins . . .

Nothing that said "seventies disco." Not even close.

He opened several websites at once, trying to find the right look. After browsing for an hour or so, he streamed a video clip of John Travolta in the film *Saturday Night Fever*. The actor's movements were graceful and hypnotic, and his formfitting white suit would be just the thing for the party.

There was a vintage clothing boutique a few blocks from Dash's penthouse apartment. He dug out the last of his weekly allowance and got into the elevator. After combing through every sale rack and trying on several outrageous outfits, he hurried back home with a large shopping bag. He took a quick shower and began getting dressed. By seven o'clock he was standing in front of the full-length mirror in his mother's room, checking the final details of his costume.

"No girl will be able to resist me tonight!" He smirked as he buttoned the vest of his three-piece

suit. He emphasized his coolness by striking a pose, with one finger pointed at the ceiling and a hand on his hip, like John Travolta doing the Hustle. To his great surprise, he pulled off the dance moves quite well.

All Dash needed was a quick spritz of cologne, and he would be ready to dance up a storm. He grabbed hold of the bottle and pumped the squirter.

"Oww!" he shouted as the cologne shot straight into his eye. "That burns like crazy!"

He ran into the bathroom to wash his face. The hot water made him cry out again. He rubbed his face harder and let out a fresh scream of pain. Finally, after what seemed like an eternity of torment, he dabbed a cool washcloth over his eye and managed to find some relief. Taking a deep breath, he opened his eye and looked at himself in the mirror. The eye looked like a fireball!

"I'm going to need a gallon of eyedrops!

The Investigation Begins . . .

"Where did Mom put them?" the young detective cried out in despair. Half-blinded, he wandered through the apartment, bumping into furniture and slipping on piles of magazines and comic books. "Maybe it's in the first-aid kit . . ."

He opened a cupboard, digging through the emergency medical kit in a frenzy. It was stuffed full of bandages, gauze, and disinfectant, but there were no eyedrops.

Meanwhile, his eyelid had gotten puffy and swollen. "I can't go to the party looking like this!" he moaned. "I have to do something!"

He paced back and forth for a few minutes. It was already well past eight o'clock, and the party would be in full swing by now. Suddenly he snapped his fingers. "I'm such an idiot!" he cried. "Why didn't I think of that sooner?"

He had come up with a solution, and even if it looked a little ridiculous, it was the best he could do in an emergency.

Twenty minutes later Dash strolled into the party, whistling as if nothing had happened. He had used styling mousse to sculpt a tuft of hair over one side of his face so that none of his friends would notice the inflamed eye hiding beneath it.

After greeting everyone, Dash scooped up an armload of snacks and found a free chair in a dark corner. All the other guests were dancing under an enormous disco ball that sent sparkling bursts of colored light around the room, but he wasn't sure if his improvised hairdo would stay in place if he started dancing.

"Aren't you going to get on the dance

The Investigation Begins . . . .

floor?" Clark asked him, shaking his hips in time to the music. "That's where all the girls are!"

Dash crossed his legs, tossing some popcorn into his mouth. "I'm saving my energy," he said, adopting a sophisticated tone. "The best dance tunes always come at the end!"

Clark chuckled, swinging his hips as he disappeared into the crowd. The disco beat set the dance floor on fire. After a fast-paced song, Mallory danced over and pulled Dash's hand. "This is my special night, Dash," she giggled. "And if you don't get up off that couch, you're going to break all the girls' hearts!"

Dash was about to reply with a sarcastic joke, but a couple of birthday well-wishers pulled Mallory to the middle of the room to cut a huge cake that had appeared out of nowhere.

In the middle of all the commotion, Dash tried to figure out his next move. *This looks like the perfect time to cut and run,* he said to himself. *I*

can use my incredible diversionary tactics to slip out while no one is watching!

But as soon as he got to his feet, he felt a light tap on his shoulder. "Are you leaving already?" asked a girl's voice. "Don't you like to party?"

Dash turned quickly and stared openmouthed at the girl who had stopped him from leaving. She was tall and willowy, with cascading blond curls and dazzling emerald eyes. She was a total fox, no doubt about it.

"I've been watching you all night long," she confessed with a nervous giggle. "I'm always

The Investigation Begins . . .

intrigued by eccentric types. Great suit, by the way." She held out her hand. "Do you have a name? I'm Linda."

"Umm . . . well . . . I'm, um, Dash," he stammered, embarrassed.

"How *dashing*! Would you like to dance?" Linda suggested.

"Umm . . . sure . . . I guess . . ."

They started to wend their way onto the dance floor. Suddenly Dash reached into his pocket, which was vibrating like mad, and pulled out an odd-looking phone. It was the state-of-the-art tech device given to Eye International students to help them carry out top secret missions around the world.

Code name: EyeNet.

Dash read the text and turned pale as a ghost. "Are you kidding me? Talk about timing!" he cried. "I need to call Agatha immediately!"

"Who's Agatha?" asked Linda, suspicious.

"She's not your girlfriend, is she?"

Dash was so worked up that he didn't even answer her. "Could I please borrow your phone? My reception is awful!" he cried.

Naturally this wasn't true, but he didn't want his teachers to intercept a call on the EyeNet and find out how much help he got with his investigations.

A moment later, he was back in the chair, sending a text to his cousin Agatha while Linda waited for him on the dance floor. As soon as he finished, he gave back her phone, apologized for the unforeseen interruption, and took off at top speed for Gatwick Airport.

A dangerous mission had just begun. Destination: the Bermuda Triangle!

A Wise Move

Agatha Mistery was twelve, two years younger than Dash and with a completely opposite personality. While her cousin was impulsive, clumsy, and madly in love with technology, Agatha was thoughtful, deliberate, and usually found with her upturned nose buried in a dusty tome.

It was no surprise that they were so different. The Mistery family tree was overloaded with a range of larger-than-life personalities who dedicated their passion and brilliance to some very unusual occupations.

Agatha kept in close touch with her relatives

all around the world, frequently gathering family news. To help keep track of them all, she recorded their contact information, professions, and other important details on an old-fashioned globe.

A few months earlier, upon their return from a scientific expedition in South Africa, Agatha's parents had noticed the globe in the living room and stood staring at her handwritten notes, wide-eyed with amazement.

"Marvelous!" her father had exclaimed, clenching his pipe between his teeth as he took quick puffs.

Her mother had rushed to hug Agatha. "Darling, we're so proud of you! I'm sorry we leave you alone so often." She sighed. "But we're always thinking of you."

"Don't worry, Mom," Agatha told her cheerfully. "Life with Watson and Chandler is never boring!"

She had turned to gaze at the other two

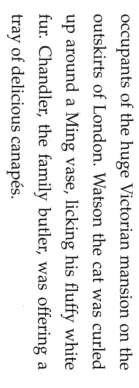

occupants of the huge Victorian mansion on the outskirts of London. Watson the cat was curled up around a Ming vase, licking his fluffy white fur. Chandler, the family butler, was offering a tray of delicious canapés.

"Extraordinary!" her father had exclaimed, leaning closer to the annotated globe.

"The World of Mistery isn't quite finished yet," Agatha told him. "I'm still updating it with some of the research I've recorded in my notebooks. It's going to take some time!"

Ever since then, she'd continued to add new details to the globe about all the far-flung and eccentric members of the Mistery family. It was a challenging task, but this didn't bother her. On the contrary, Agatha enjoyed the hard work. Her favorite pastime was digging up clues, and she hoped to become a world-famous mystery writer one day.

That Saturday night after dinner, she was

sitting at the desk in her bedroom consulting a mountain of books and taking notes. Watson played on the bed, batting around an increasingly frayed ball of yarn. A soft knock sounded at the door, and Agatha stopped writing. "Is everything ready, Chandler?" she asked as the butler entered the room.

"Just as you ordered, Miss," he replied.

"The luggage is packed?"

"Certainly, Miss."

"And Watson's carrier?"

"It's in the trunk of the limousine."

"Good job. I'll be down in a minute!"

Agatha put on a necklace and two silver bracelets, then brushed her blond hair. The evening dress she wore was gray cashmere with lace trim—very expensive. She was going to the Theatre Royal, the most elegant theater in London, and she had to look the part!

Stroking her small, upturned nose, she

turned toward Watson. "Do you promise to behave yourself?" she whispered. "If they find you hiding in my purse, we'll be in all sorts of trouble."

In response, the cat jumped into her purse and lay perfectly still. Agatha gave him a grateful pat on the head and started down the stairs.

When they arrived at the car, Chandler held the door open for her. Even he had dressed up:

a double-breasted mauve suit with a blue silk scarf in place of his usual dinner jacket. Only his bearlike stature and flattened nose betrayed his past as a professional heavyweight boxer.

"Don't forget to activate the burglar alarm," Agatha reminded him. "I have a feeling we're going to be gone for a while."

Chandler activated the alarm system with a remote control and rubbed his square jaw. "What

makes you so sure Master Dash will be calling tonight?" he questioned.

That afternoon, Agatha had suggested that they pack their bags "just in case." She was convinced Dash was about to lure them away on another investigative mission. Knowing his young mistress's incredible intuition, Chandler had obeyed without batting an eye.

"I'm playing the odds," replied Agatha with a smile. "I have two good reasons for thinking so. First, it's been more than a month since his last mission. It seems strange that Eye International would leave him inactive for so long."

"I see," said the butler. "So we'll have to help him solve a crime in some obscure part of the world?"

"As usual," she replied.

"And the second reason, Miss?"

Agatha turned to look at him. "Well, isn't it obvious? Tonight we have tickets for my favorite

A Wise Move

play, Shakespeare's *Hamlet*, and Dash is an expert at interrupting my plans!"

Chandler let out a dry laugh and started to drive with smooth confidence.

At a quarter past eight, they left the limousine keys with the valet at the Theatre Royal, a grand white building in a neoclassical style. London's high society filed through its doors in a slow, twittering procession.

"I booked us a box," the girl whispered to Chandler as she handed the usher their tickets.

"Hurry up, I can hear Watson clawing the inside of my purse!"

They slipped into their private box on the second floor. Chandler closed its door firmly, and Agatha let the cat out of his hiding place.

In an instant, Watson jumped onto Agatha's knee and gazed around, pricking his ears.

There was a magical atmosphere in the theater. A huge chandelier with thousands of

bulbs hung from the ornate ceiling.

The lights dimmed, and the audience's chattering softened until there was total silence.

The curtain opened, and there was a round of applause.

The first scene showed the crenellated ramparts of a stone castle, where two terrified guards encountered the ghost of their dead king. Then Hamlet, Prince of Denmark, took center stage, swearing to his father that he'd take revenge on his murderer.

Even though she knew every line by heart, Agatha was hypnotized by the beauty of Shakespeare's language. But the magic was soon interrupted by a vibrating phone.

The butler peeked at the screen, then handed it to her with a resigned expression. "You were right, Miss Agatha," he whispered. "Looks like a message from Master Dash . . ."

Agatha read her cousin's text:

AGENT DM14 HERE. GO STRAIGHT TO GATWICK AIRPORT AND TAKE THE NEXT BRITISH AIRWAYS FLIGHT TO BERMUDA. P.S. IF YOU DON'T COME, I'M SUNK!

Agatha gave Chandler a smile; her intuition had been right again! She grabbed her purse, stepped out of the box, and set off down the Theatre Royal's luxurious halls, while Watson and Chandler followed closely behind. They reached the exit in moments, and soon the limousine was speeding out of the garage.

On the way to the airport, the girl thought aloud. "If my memory serves me correctly, we have a relative in Bermuda—an uncle," she muttered, flipping through the pages of her notebook. "But how can I reach him?"

It wasn't until they were in the check-in line that she discovered a tiny note penciled in one of the margins.

"Here it is!" she exclaimed, beaming. "Uncle

Conrad, and here is his phone number! I'll call him before we take off."

"There are just a few minutes until our departure," objected the butler. "Master Dash will be beside himself . . ."

Agatha quickly ducked out of the line, dialing the number. A moment later, she was chatting with Conrad Mistery on the other side of the Atlantic Ocean.

The Bermuda Triangle

"I was about to give up hope!" Dash exclaimed with a grin as he saw Agatha, Chandler, and Watson approaching the gate. Then he turned to the flight attendant who was helping the boarding passengers. "What did I tell you? We Misterys always keep our word!"

The attendant nodded. "Next time, Mr. Mistery, I'd lose the Halloween costume," he replied.

Agatha and Chandler could barely hold back their laughter. In his fitted disco outfit with a tuft of hair moussed over one eye, Dash looked like he had stepped out of a retro music video.

The boy grunted at the flight attendant, and Agatha put a hand on his arm. "Let's go find our seats, Dash," she said amiably. "We're dying to hear more about this mission."

The young detective followed her, still grumbling. Whenever he started a new investigation, his fear of failure made him anxious and cranky. He slumped into his seat, staring out the window. "Darn it, she was the cutest girl in the world . . ." He sighed. "How am I going to see her again?"

The Boeing 777 roared upward into the night sky. Agatha waited for Dash to finish muttering, then asked in a teasing voice, "What's her name, this new flame of yours?"

"Umm . . . I think it was Linda," he mumbled. "And what did Linda think of your swollen eye?"

Dash jolted in his seat, reaching to see if his hair had moved. "How did you know?" he

The Bermuda Triangle

asked, surprised. Then he hunched his shoulders, grumbling, "You never miss a trick!"

"You need some eyedrops," she advised, rummaging in her purse. "If your eye gets infected, it'll really hurt!"

With Chandler's help, Agatha doctored Dash's eye. Watson waved his tail every time the boy squealed—it was well-known that the cat wasn't a fan of Agatha's cousin. When she had finished, the young detective found himself with a fancy gauze patch over one eye.

"You look like a fierce buccaneer, Cap'n Dash."

Agatha chuckled. "Ready to fearlessly take on the perils of the Bermuda Triangle!"

Dash gave her a one-eyed glare, but before he could speak, Chandler asked

politely, "Can you give us a few details about this investigation, Master Dash?"

"Um, I don't really have much of a clue," he confessed. "I was waiting until we were all together to listen to the briefing . . ."

"Go ahead, dear cousin," said Agatha.

Dash pulled out his EyeNet and handed wireless earbuds to his colleagues. He pushed a sequence of buttons, and his professor of Espionage and Counterespionage appeared on the screen. He was a young-looking man with a voice like a duck.

"Good evening, DM14," the professor quacked. "You have been chosen to work on a delicate investigation for a Mr. Ronald McBain. Do you know that name?" the professor asked with significant emphasis. Dash put the recording on PAUSE.

"Do we know whom he's referring to?" he asked the others uncertainly.

The Bermuda Triangle

"Who doesn't?" Agatha said with a smile. "He's the McBain of McBain's Fresh Fish, the fish-and-chips chain. Chandler and I eat there sometimes."

"They have an excellent batter," the butler confirmed. "Very crispy."

Dash's mouth started to water.

"If my memory serves me correctly," Agatha continued, "Mr. McBain is Australian and has a fleet of fishing boats in every corner of the ocean."

"Okay, so he's a big fish," Dash commented, wrinkling his forehead. "But what's a fast-food billionaire doing in the Bermuda Triangle?"

"Let's continue with the briefing and find out!"

Dash pressed PLAY on the recording, and the professor continued speaking on the small screen. But the information he provided did little to clear up their questions.

Ronald McBain wanted to maintain utmost

secrecy and would only reveal the mission details to the Eye International agent in person, at his luxury villa.

"Your appointment with Mr. McBain is at nine o'clock tomorrow morning," concluded the professor. "Best of luck, Agent DM14!" And with a flash on the screen, he disappeared.

Dash gripped the armrest in desperation. "Is that all?" he exclaimed, scrolling frantically through the file menu. "No other files?"

Agatha was pensive. "Hmm, this is a very strange case," she commented.

Chandler limited his opinion to a slight cough.

They passed the next few minutes in silence, lulled by the hum of the plane's engines. It was the first time they'd ever begun an investigation with so little to go on.

"Try not to worry," Agatha soothed Dash. "We'll find out everything we need to know

The Bermuda Triangle

tomorrow! In the meantime, let's pool our knowledge about our destination."

Dash perked up instantly. "Aha!" he exclaimed. "This time I can open one of *my* memory drawers!"

"What do you mean, young sir?" asked Chandler.

"I've done tons of research on the Bermuda Triangle," Dash said. He took out a piece of paper and drew a small map. "The points of the triangle are the coast of Florida, the island of Puerto Rico, and the Bermuda archipelago, which is made up of more than one hundred islands. Over the past several centuries, a huge number of boats and airplanes have disappeared there without a trace . . ."

His companions let him rant for a while about conspiracy theories, alien abductions, and paranormal phenomena, until Agatha interrupted him with a quick question. "Do

you know the first person to report strange occurrences in the triangle?"

"Umm . . . no," Dash admitted.

"Believe it or not, Christopher Columbus noted mysterious lights in the sky during his voyage to America," she replied.

Dash looked crushed. "You're just too smart," he muttered.

They continued to chat for a few more minutes until, overcome with exhaustion, they all drifted off to sleep.

The captain's amplified voice awoke them. "Fasten your seat belts, we're about to land in Bermuda!"

Peering out the window, they saw a lone, hook-shaped island emerge from the dark ocean waters.

Dash's retro outfit gave the customs officials a good laugh as he left the plane. He ignored them, trailing behind his companions until he

was stopped in his tracks by a hearty slap on the back.

"Hey, kids!" their uncle Conrad greeted them enthusiastically. "You're right on time!" Bulging with muscles, he had deeply tanned skin and a very white smile. "Hey, are you in the fashion business?" he joked. "I've never seen such style!"

"Uncle Conrad, it's great to see you!" cried Agatha. "You're the very picture of good health!"

"Fresh air, warm sun, and plenty of exercise." Conrad Mistery grinned. "So what brings you three to Bermuda?"

"Well . . . Dash is doing research for a school project," Agatha said. It was almost the truth.

"Cool! You can tell me the details whenever you're ready," their uncle replied. "Now let's get home for some rest. You must be exhausted after the trip."

"I could sleep for a month," yawned the young detective.

"Dash has sloth genes," said Agatha.

"More energy, boy!" Conrad said, slapping his back again. "We'll get you out in the fresh air and sunshine! Come on, follow me!"

The night air was balmy and sweet after a wintry London. They boarded a pink-and-blue bus that had very few passengers, and ten minutes later, Conrad led them off the bus in front of a brightly lit sign that read MISTERY WATER PARK.

"Wh-where are we?" asked Dash, staring in wonder at the neon shape of a dolphin.

Uncle Conrad opened the gate. "This is my place, dear nephew! I own and operate this water park!"

"It's fantastic!" breathed Agatha, in seventh heaven. She had already researched her uncle's profession, but she never could have imagined all the pools, waterslides, Jet Skis, and sailboats moored alongside the beach.

The Bermuda Triangle

"Glad you like it." He beamed. "Come on, I'll introduce you to my star attractions!" They followed him out to a vast, softly lit pool. "Look, kids, and tell me they aren't true beauties!"

Five dolphins swam through the calm water.

Agatha crouched down at the edge of the pool, and one of the dolphins immediately ventured closer. The girl reached out to touch its head, and the dolphin gave a whistle of happiness.

CHAPTER TWO

"That means he likes you," explained Uncle Conrad. "But no time to make friends now. It's time for bed! You've got a beautiful island to see in the morning!"

He escorted the three Londoners into the main building, where they fell asleep in their beds within minutes.

CHAPTER THREE

Close Encounter with a Shark

$\mathcal{T}$he Bermuda sun was already high in the sky when the aspiring detectives awoke. Agatha bounced out of bed, ready to devour a delicious breakfast of tropical fruits, while Dash sluggishly trailed behind, grumbling about wanting more sleep. Their uncle had raided the water park's souvenir shop to find more appropriate clothes for the warm island climate. Dash and Agatha proudly wore their new Mistery Water Park T-shirts, while Chandler sported a flamboyant floral shirt and a pair of sandals.

"Now, what do you say to a tour on my yacht?" asked Conrad, who seemed to have energy bursting from every pore. "I'll take you to the most magical place in the world: the coral reef!"

"That's very kind of you," Agatha said with a smile. "But there's something we've got to do first."

Uncle Conrad looked confused. "Wouldn't you rather swim with the dolphins? Or take a water safari on Jet Skis?" he asked. "There's a world of fun here. The choice is yours!"

"I need to interview someone for my assignment," sighed Dash, who had pulled up his eye patch at the mention of a safari to stare greedily at the Jet Skis.

"Who is it? I know everyone on the island!"

"His name's Ronald McBain," Chandler replied.

Uncle Conrad was stunned. "What?" he cried.

"McBain the Shark?"

"What a graphic nickname," Chandler said, raising his eyebrows.

"McBain is kind of a local celebrity," Conrad explained, joining them at the table. He didn't look happy. "He moved to Bermuda some years ago. This island is an international tax haven, you know, so McBain bought a spectacular villa where he can enjoy his billions in peace."

"Why do you call him the Shark?" Agatha started stroking her nose, intrigued.

"Everyone knows McBain has a passion for salvaging ancient shipwrecks. But what interests him even more is their cargo: gold, coins, precious jewels. They say he'll stop at nothing to get what he wants."

Dash elbowed his cousin. "Maybe that's why he contacted Eye International," he whispered in her ear. "A stolen treasure!"

She nodded, then turned back to Conrad. "Could you please tell us the quickest way to get to his villa?" she asked.

Conrad marked the route on a postcard of the

island and escorted them to the water park's exit. "Be careful around that man," he called out as they walked away. "You can't trust a shark."

Chandler nodded, flexing his knuckles.

They took a bus along wide streets lined with palm trees and emerald-green grass. Even though it was past the holiday tourist season, there was a steady stream of cars, bikes, and brightly colored motor scooters. It took just a few minutes to reach the capital city of Hamilton, its streets lined with pastel-painted colonial buildings.

Ronald McBain's estate was not far from the city center. A high fence encircled a sumptuous two-story villa surrounded by palm trees and flowers. The entry gate framed a view of broad steps leading onto a wraparound deck and infinity pool.

On one side of the building, there was a small pier overlooking the ocean, and on the other, a private heliport.

Close Encounter with a Shark

Agatha introduced herself and the rest of their group to the two bodyguards stationed in front of the gate. One of the men spoke into his phone before giving them a nod to enter. McBain was waiting impatiently for them on the veranda.

He was a heavyset older man with a thick white beard. His eyes were as hard as steel. He was dressed in a white suit and stylish panama hat. He welcomed his guests cordially, but seemed very surprised by the group that faced him. "You certainly make an unlikely team!" he said, looking them over. "Are all of you agents?"

Agatha smiled in response. "Aside from Watson, you can count on any of us!"

Still skeptical, McBain barked out a sharp laugh and invited them into his study. The window looked out over a swimming pool carved directly into the rocky ground.

"Mr. McBain?" Agatha asked, professionally. "Could you please explain why we're here?"

"Good. I like to cut to the chase," he replied, leaning his elbows on the desk. He continued, "As you may have heard, I'm an aficionado of shipwrecks . . ."

"Yes, we already knew that," Dash interrupted.

"It's our job to do background checks."

McBain paused for a moment, staring at the patch covering Dash's eye, then continued. "For several years now, I've been searching for the *Alcazar*, a Spanish galleon that transported gold bullion from Mexico in the days of the

conquistadores. But this ship wasn't like all the rest. It had a one-of-a-kind cargo . . ."

"Could you be more precise, Mr. McBain?" asked Agatha, opening her notebook and resting it on her knee.

"According to the ship's log, the *Alcazar* had a precious Mayan calendar on board," the elderly billionaire said. "A golden disk, nearly a yard in diameter . . ."

"A priceless relic," interjected Chandler, petting Watson to keep him calm.

"Priceless doesn't begin to describe it!" McBain snorted, fixing him with a challenging glare. "Once I discovered that the galleon had sunk off the coast of Bermuda, I immediately hired Captain Larsson and his crew. Olaf Larsson is an old Norwegian sea dog who's spent his whole life recovering shipwrecks. I invested a fortune outfitting his ship, the *Loki*, with state-of-the-art deep-sea research equipment. After months

scanning the depths of the ocean, the captain finally located the remains of the *Alcazar* . . ."

McBain paused to evaluate his guests' reactions. Then he got right to the point. "The crew finally managed to haul up the Mayan calendar, but they lost it again a few nights ago. Don't you find that strange, detectives? That is why I contacted Eye International."

They exchanged knowing looks, leaving Agatha to reply.

"Could you tell us exactly what happened?" she asked, lightly tapping her nose with her pen.

"That night, the *Loki* was caught in a terrible storm. There was a lot of damage." McBain sighed. "Captain Larsson called me on the satellite phone to say that the Mayan calendar had fallen overboard during the storm. But I think that Norwegian crook is trying to rob me!"

"Why? What makes you think so?" asked Dash.

Close Encounter with a Shark

—

McBain gave a toothy smile, resting his hands on his prominent belly. "When I hired Captain Larsson, I promised him half of the money from the sale of whatever we could recover. With all his years of experience, it's inconceivable that he'd lose the most valuable find of his whole treasure-hunting career in a mere storm at sea!"

"Excuse me," Agatha interrupted him. "But if I recall correctly, there are international laws prohibiting private sales of this sort of cultural relic."

"Sure, there are," replied McBain with a fiendish grin. "But no one would have known who discovered it. I could have told the auction houses in London and New York any story that came into my head."

This admission left the three investigators at a loss for words. It was clear why McBain was known as the Shark.

"So you believe Larsson orchestrated a scam

to keep the relic himself?" Chandler asked.

The elderly billionaire's expression darkened.

"Exactly, detectives. Your task is to find out where Larsson is hiding the treasure, and catch him red-handed!"

"I don't understand," replied Agatha, chewing her lip. "Was the captain the only person who knew about the Mayan calendar? Couldn't there be other suspects?"

"Naturally the crew knew everything, but I don't think any of them would be able to pull off putting such an important artifact on the market," McBain replied coldly. "It's not a fool's game."

Agatha wasn't convinced. "Other than your suspicions, I don't see anything that would indicate that the captain's a thief," she observed.

"I'm pleased to see you're such a clever one, Miss," said the unscrupulous billionaire. "I will confess that I took . . . certain other precautions.

Close Encounter with a Shark

I have a man on board the *Loki*. His name is Richie Stark, and he oversees all the electronic equipment. He is also convinced that the captain has hidden the calendar somewhere."

"A spy!" Dash exclaimed.

"I'd call him more of an insurance policy," McBain said with a crafty grin.

Once again, the three detectives were stunned by McBain's icy attitude. After a few awkward moments, Agatha got to her feet. "We have a good grasp of the situation," she said, pacing back and forth. "But with your permission, I'd like to ask you a few more simple questions."

He invited her to go on with an eloquent wave of his hand.

"First off," began the girl. "Why weren't you overseeing this operation in person?"

"I suffer terribly from seasickness," McBain replied grimly. "Ironic, no? I always travel by private jet and helicopter. Not only are they

more comfortable for me, but they are faster, and speed is essential to running my business affairs. I expect speedy results from you, too," he added.

"Of course," said Agatha, nodding. "Secondly, where will we find the *Loki*?"

"It's anchored about fifty nautical miles south of Bermuda." He opened a desk drawer and pulled out a couple of pages. "Here are the coordinates and a full list of the crew members," he said, standing. As far as he was concerned, their meeting was over. "My yacht is moored outside, ready to take you there."

Agatha shook her head. "We'd rather use Eye International resources," she insisted. "We'll be in touch soon, Mr. McBain."

The three investigators shook the elderly magnate's hand and left the villa in silence.

A Storm to End All Storms

$\mathscr{A}$s they all walked back to the bus stop, Chandler surveyed the ocean. "What Eye International resources?" he asked, worried. "What do you mean, Miss Agatha?"

"I get the distinct feeling McBain is hiding something," replied Agatha. "His men could interfere with our investigation."

"So how do you intend to get us to the *Loki*?" Dash interrupted, unnerved.

A flash of cleverness lit up Agatha's eyes. "Simple. We'll get Uncle Conrad to take us!"

Dash grumbled all the way back, but in the end he agreed that telling their uncle the real

reason for their trip was the right thing to do.

When they got back to the water park, Conrad was crouched by the edge of the pool, throwing sardines in the air. The dolphins jumped up and grabbed them in midair as they did spectacular somersaults.

Trying to avoid getting soaked by the spray, Agatha and Dash told him everything, not missing a single detail.

"If I can't solve this case, I'm washed up," Dash groaned, dejected.

"Aha!" exclaimed their uncle, thumping Dash's back. "A budding detective! I knew there was no such thing as a Mistery with sloth DNA!" He flexed his muscles and grinned. "Ready to go, kids?"

Within moments they were on board his yacht. After warming up the engine, the boat chugged out of the turquoise lagoon, carefully navigating between dry, rocky outcrops.

A Storm to End All Storms

"Hey, kids!" shouted Conrad, raising one hand from the wheel to point. "There's a sight for you northerners. Look over there!"

Agatha and Dash turned toward a stunning sight. A stretch of beach, curving between the rocks, shimmered rose-pink in the midday sun.

"Pink sand?" said Dash, stunned. "How is that possible?"

Leaning against the rail, Agatha unleashed her prodigious memory once more. "If my memory serves me correctly, that's the magnificent Horseshoe Bay," she explained. "The powdered remains of ancient seashells make the sand that incredible color."

"Well-done!" roared Uncle Conrad. "Why don't you move here and become a tour guide?" Chandler just raised an eyebrow.

Thirty minutes later, the yacht was heading due south, and their uncle put it on autopilot.

He invited Dash and Agatha to follow him down a set of steps into the hold, where he pushed a button on an electronic dashboard. With a soft buzz, the metal bulkheads slid into the sides of

the boat, revealing huge underwater windows. "This is one of the world's most unique ways to observe a coral reef!" he announced proudly, tapping his hand on the transparent panels. "Tempered and reinforced plexiglass!"

The silent realm of the coral reef spread out before them, giving the sensation that they were gliding along the ocean floor. Multicolored tropical fish swam in and out of the coral and hid in the masses of seaweed that rippled like ribbons in the current. Even Watson seemed to enjoy the view, stretching out his paw to grab some illusory prey.

Conrad returned to the helm, asking Chandler to help him with the ropes. Dash and Agatha

remained below to admire the neon-bright tropical fish darting past as a sinister-looking moray eel lurked inside a ravine.

Finally Agatha managed to tear herself away from the glorious view. "All right, cousin, let's get to work," she suggested, taking a seat. "I've been thinking about this case, and I have a few doubts . . . Are you with me?"

"I'm listening," Dash said, his good eye still glued to the ocean outside. "Go ahead!"

"I'm wondering if Mr. McBain didn't *want* us to pick up too much information," Agatha whispered. "Maybe he stole the Mayan calendar himself, so he wouldn't have to divide the profits with the captain or anyone else."

"How could he have done that? He wasn't on board the *Loki*," Dash objected. "Oh wait—he told us he has a spy on the crew! Maybe Richie Stark stole it for him!"

"But if that were the case, why would McBain

have told us he had an informant?" Agatha asked. She shook her head. "I have to admit, it really bothers me that we're conducting an investigation for an unscrupulous shark like McBain. If we find the calendar and give it back to him, we'd become accomplices in his crime."

Dash scratched his head. "What's the right thing to do, then?" he asked. "Should we—"

"I just don't know," Agatha cut him off. "Let's take a look at the list of crew members. Maybe that will give us some ideas."

The *Loki*'s crew was made up of Captain Olaf Larsson; Raul Santiago, the boatswain; Davey O'Connor, the steward; Richie Stark, the electronics technician and McBain's right hand; and two scuba divers, identical twins named Ramona and Ramira Sanchez. Dash pulled out his EyeNet and searched through Eye International's vast archives for information. None of them had a criminal record.

He and Agatha committed their photos and any pertinent career information to memory. The real rookie of the group was Richie Stark—this was his first salvage mission.

After three hours at sea, the *Loki* loomed on the horizon. It was a compact oceanographic ship, bristling with antennas, and it had a large winch and pulley system on the bow, designed for hauling up heavy objects from the ocean floor. The cabin was badly in need of a fresh coat of paint, and the rest of the boat looked as if it could use some attention, too.

Uncle Conrad got on the marine radio, requesting

permission to dock. The yacht pulled in and gently berthed alongside the *Loki.*

A tall, strapping figure stepped forward. "By a thousand whalers, who be you?" he grunted suspiciously. His untrimmed beard and shaggy blond ponytail gave him the look of an authentic pirate.

"Mr. McBain sent us to investigate the incident during the storm, Captain Larsson," said Agatha, who recognized him from his picture.

"What does that old vulture want?" roared the captain.

"He wants to know exactly what happened to the Mayan calendar," Dash said.

"So that useless scavenger told you his secret! What else did he tell you, for Blackbeard's sake?"

"He was more interested in what you could tell us," replied Agatha with a smile.

Larsson burst out laughing and strode toward the bridge, gesturing for them to follow.

CHAPTER FOUR

He leaned against the control panel and began talking angrily. "We hauled up the calendar that afternoon, after a lot of hard work. The blasted thing weighed a ton, but we finally managed to hoist it on board and brought it up to the bow, where we laid it out on a tarp and secured it to the deck with steel bars."

"Are you sure it was secured correctly?" Dash interrupted, hoping to solve the case as soon as possible by declaring it an accident.

"I don't make mistakes, kid," barked Larsson, pointing his finger in Dash's face.

Dash took a step back. "Um, it was just a theory," he muttered, intimidated.

Larsson glared at him for a moment before continuing. "Since it was already late in the day and the sea was beginning to get choppy, we decided to wait until morning to clean up the relic. We knew there was bad weather brewing, but we underestimated the strength of the storm.

The wind blew us off course, the rain came down by the bucketload, and there were waves as high as three-story buildings, by the walrus's tusks!"

Agatha was entertained by his colorful expressions. "Captain, what were you doing when the storm hit your boat?" she asked, taking notes in her notebook.

"I was right here on the bridge. Then Ramona Sanchez came up to warn me that the hold had sprung a leak and O'Connor needed my help."

"Are you sure it was Ramona?" asked Agatha. The photos of the twins in the file were identical.

"That's who she said she was. I haven't learned how to tell them apart yet."

"What happened in the hold?"

"I helped O'Connor man the bilge pumps; we were taking on water. It was backbreaking work. When O'Connor told me he could finish

the job on his own, I returned to the helm. That was when I noticed that the calendar was gone."

"What happened next, captain?" Chandler asked politely.

"I went to check what had happened. The straps that secured the calendar to the steel bars had come loose, which didn't really surprise me. By that time the storm was really violent, and the ship had tilted dangerously a few times."

Agatha was watching his eyes very closely, trying to assess the truthfulness of his story.

"Where were the other crew members while you were manning the pumps?" she asked.

"I couldn't tell you for sure," he replied. "But as soon as I saw that the calendar was missing, I went below deck and found Santiago there with the Sanchez twins, all of them shivering in their wet raincoats. O'Connor was still bailing out the hold, and that landlubber Richie Stark

spent the whole time holed up inside his lab."

"Was there anything else missing?" Agatha pressed him.

"I'll say! Santiago informed me the AUV had sunk, and then we discovered the lifeboat had blown out to sea."

"AUV? What's that?" asked Dash.

"Walrus tusks, are you all amateurs?" cried Larsson. "AUV—*autonomous underwater vehicle*. It's a robot for underwater research!"

"What does it do?" asked Agatha, always curious.

Uncle Conrad answered before the captain could. "It's an underwater probe; you enter in coordinates and it searches the ocean floor by itself," he explained. "It has instruments for collecting all sorts of data."

"It was the AUV that located the calendar," rasped the captain. "Richie was operating it. If you want to know more, you'll have to ask him."

"We'll do that." Agatha nodded decisively. "For now, would you mind if we make a quick search of the *Loki*?"

The captain agreed to her request. Who could say no to her clever smile?

CHAPTER FIVE

Traces of Sabotage

$\mathcal{A}$s they climbed back down to the deck, Larsson told them that after the calendar's disappearance, he had tried to contact McBain, but the marine radio didn't work. Nor did the radar or the Fathometer.

"That's a lot of damage," Chandler remarked.

"You're telling me," groaned the captain. "The *Loki* is an old vessel, and she's always served me well, but she's reached her limits. With the money that I would have earned from this job, I could have finally bought a whole new boat. Bad luck haunts me, by Blackbeard's soul!" He suddenly stopped in his tracks. "There's something I have to take care of. Do whatever searching you need to do and be done with it," he grumbled. Then he returned to the bridge without saying good-bye.

Agatha and Dash made their way to the bow, their uncle and Chandler behind them. Watson romped along happily, curious about this totally new environment. As they approached the winch, they could clearly hear the ringing of an enormous hammer.

The silhouette of an immense sailor seemed to block out the sun. He was even taller than Chandler. Sweat glistened on his shaved head, and his dark skin revealed his Cuban ancestry, just as the agency's file had reported. A gleaming machete hung from his belt, and he wore a sweat-stained T-shirt and shorts.

Raul Santiago scanned the newcomers with a suspicious frown, and Agatha hurried to explain their reason for being on board.

"Storm came, storm went," replied the bulky

Traces of Sabotage

boatswain, returning to his hammering.

"Mr. McBain told us about the Mayan calendar," Agatha said politely. "We'd be very grateful if you could tell us what you were doing during the storm."

Santiago put the hammer down, wiping the sweat from his brow. "When the storm started tossing the boat around and the captain went below, I went up to the bridge to make sure the

boat stayed on course." He stopped abruptly to glare at Watson, who was weaving in and out of his legs. "Hey, is that your nuisance?" he growled.

Uncle Conrad knelt down to scratch the Siberian cat's head. "Come on, Watson, why don't you go for a little walk," he suggested gently. The cat stalked away, tail straight and expression offended.

"Was the calendar still in its place?" Dash continued.

"I checked it myself. It was strapped down securely."

"What happened after that?" asked Agatha.

"How long did you stay on the bridge?"

"Not very long. The storm got worse fast. I was heading back below deck when I heard the crash."

"What crash?" interrupted Chandler.

"This winch." Santiago pointed at a broken pulley in front of them. "There was a loud bang

and the AUV sank within seconds."

"How can you be sure? Did you see it go down?" Agatha wanted to know.

"No, I just heard the noise. Maybe it was a rogue wave or the wind that pushed it into the sea. The AUV was attached to the boat by two metal cables. When I got back up here, one cable had snapped, but the other was still holding fast. The shock must have been pretty strong, because the whole pulley was bent around to one side—see?"

Santiago picked up his hammer. "And now I need to finish bending it back, if you don't mind . . ."

"Is it possible for the AUV to sink that fast?" asked Uncle Conrad. "Doesn't it have a flotation system?"

The boatswain had clearly had enough. "Look, the thing sank, okay? Who knows where those giant waves took it. We searched and

searched the ocean floor, but there's no trace of it anywhere." He paused again. "That cat of yours is a real pest, you know?"

Watson had knocked over a slop bucket. A mass of fresh fish spilled out over the deck, and he yowled with delight, anticipating the snack of a lifetime.

"Chandler, could you please grab Watson before he does any more damage?" asked Agatha.

The butler obeyed immediately. Watson squirmed in his arms as the girl went on questioning Santiago. "What happened after the crash?"

"I battened down the pulley. I was scared it might get damaged beyond repair. Once I'd taken care of that, I went below deck to get out of the rain."

"Did you see anybody else on deck while you were up here?"

"I was working too hard to admire the view,"

he said with a sarcastic grin. "You think someone stole that calendar, don't you? Or is that what McBain thinks?"

"It seems like quite a coincidence that the calendar was finally found, then immediately disappeared in a storm," replied Dash. "Don't you find that odd, Santiago?"

"Actually, boy, I don't think it was a coincidence at all!"

Agatha tapped the tip of her nose. "So you think it was stolen, too?" she ventured.

"No," thundered the man. "It was Yemaya."

Dash looked around. "Who is that? Another crew member?" He seemed confused.

"My dear cousin, Yemaya is the Caribbean goddess of the sea," replied Agatha, tapping her pen against her notebook. "Perhaps you should explain what you mean, Señor Santiago."

The huge sailor grabbed hold of the pulley, hitting it hard with his hammer. "It was Yemaya

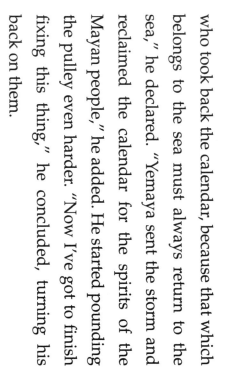

who took back the calendar, because that which belongs to the sea must always return to the sea," he declared. "Yemaya sent the storm and reclaimed the calendar for the spirits of the Mayan people," he added. He started pounding the pulley even harder. "Now I've got to finish fixing this thing," he concluded, turning his back on them.

Agatha noticed that Chandler was trying to get her attention. He was standing next to a large stack of crates, with Watson pinned in his arms.

The girl gestured to Dash and Conrad to follow her. "What's going on?" she asked the butler.

The jack-of-all-trades of the Mistery House pointed at something poking out from behind one of the crates. "Miss, I just spotted this stub of metal cable. I thought it might interest you."

Agatha bent down to examine it. It was

identical to the cable that Santiago had described to them.

"The other cable from the AUV," muttered Dash.

"Looks that way," Agatha said. "But don't you think there's something strange about it?"

The young detective examined the cable, trying to figure out what she meant.

"The end isn't frayed, but severed cleanly," said Chandler.

"Are you saying it was cut on purpose?" asked Dash.

"It would seem so," whispered Agatha. "Which means we have a new clue to follow!"

Just then, they heard a noise from behind them. A female figure in a wet suit and scuba-diving gear was climbing over the side of the boat onto the deck, followed by another figure of the same build.

"Quick, let's go take a look!" exclaimed

Agatha. "For now, whatever we find needs to stay between us." She led her companions to the middle of the boat, watching the two young women as they clambered onto the deck.

They took off their masks and mouthpieces, then started helping each other unfasten the heavy oxygen tanks from their shoulders.

"The Sanchez sisters, I presume?" asked Agatha, walking toward them.

Both sisters had short, jet-black hair, full mouths, and shiny, dark eyes. Their wet suits clung to strong bodies, sculpted by constant diving.

"Excuse me, but who are you?" asked one of the twins, sharing a puzzled look with her sister.

Agatha briefly explained why they were on board.

"So old Sharkface suspects something fishy is going on," sighed the twin who introduced herself as Ramira.

"He's probably looking for a scapegoat," said her sister, Ramona.

Uncle Conrad flashed them both a flirtatious smile. "Ladies, can I give you a hand with those heavy tanks?" he asked gallantly.

"Not now, Uncle," whispered Agatha, winking at him. She turned back to the twins. "If you have a minute, we'd like to hear where you were on the night of the storm," she explained.

"There isn't much to tell," replied Ramira. "We were below deck, in our cabin. There wasn't anything much we could do to help out. The captain was at the helm, Richie was in his lab, and O'Connor was in the hold."

"And Santiago was outside on deck," concluded Ramona. "We decided it would be best to stay in our cabin, where it was warm and dry, and check out our diving equipment for the next day."

"You didn't go up on deck at all?" asked

Agatha, checking her notebook.

"Well, I did," replied Ramira. "O'Connor came out of the hold, saying there was a leak and he needed the captain's help, so I offered to go up and fetch him."

Dash shot a significant glance at his cousin.

"But the captain said it was Ramona who came looking for him," he said.

"He was wrong," said Ramona, shrugging. "As you can see, we're as alike as two drops of water."

A lightbulb lit up in Agatha's mind. "So what did you do?" she asked the twins.

"When the captain followed me down from the bridge, I went back to my sister and we continued our work," said Ramira. "Then Santiago came below deck, soaking wet, and we fixed him some hot herbal tea and chatted for a while."

Her sister nodded. "Till the captain came

back, yelling like a madman because the Mayan calendar had disappeared into the sea."

Agatha elbowed her cousin discreetly. "There's something that doesn't sit right with their version of events," she whispered. "Add the Sanchez sisters to our list of suspects."

The Hole in the Hull

"If you don't need anything else right now, we're going to go hose off this salt water," chirped Ramira. "We've got another dive to prepare for."

Agatha glanced at the pulley, which Santiago was still trying to hammer back into shape. "Are you trying to locate the AUV?" she asked.

"No, we've given up on that. We're surveying the perimeter of the wreck zone . . . ," Ramona began, and her twin sister jumped in to finish her sentence. It was as if one person was speaking.

" . . . because the captain wants to recover the gold coins the AUV found in the wreck . . . ," continued Ramira.

" . . . but the storm shook everything up down there, too . . ."

" . . . and without the AUV's magnetometer, the only way to locate the doubloons is by eye!"

"Okay, that's all we need for now." Agatha nodded. "We'll keep you updated."

The twins collected their scuba gear and headed for their bunks. Ramira patted Watson's head while Ramona winked at Uncle Conrad, who immediately responded with a winning smile.

When they had gone below deck, Dash asked, "So, cousin, what's your intuition telling you?"

Agatha thought for a moment, her eyes fixed on the calm sea. "Remember when the captain said that he found the twins wearing wet raincoats?"

"Yes, what about it?"

"The Sanchez sisters said no such thing," whispered Agatha. "They said they were down

in their cabin keeping dry. What if instead of staying below deck during the storm, they were really up above?"

"The captain could be lying," said Chandler impassively.

"That's true," Agatha admitted. "But Larsson wouldn't have made up a lie that could be disproved so easily. And besides that—"

"I bet you're thinking about the strange case of mistaken identity between Ramira and Ramona. Right, cousin?" Dash jumped in.

Agatha nodded. "Exactly. Why would the captain have pretended that he was confused?"

"So to sum up," said Dash, "the Sanchez sisters are definitely hiding something!"

Uncle Conrad leaned on the ship's railing and sighed, looking dreamy. "But two such bewitching and beautiful girls . . . I can't imagine them getting caught up in something so shady," he objected.

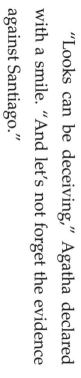

"Looks can be deceiving," Agatha declared with a smile. "And let's not forget the evidence against Santiago."

"The severed AUV cable!" cried Dash.

"You would need a very sharp tool to cut a cable like that one," agreed Uncle Conrad with a shiver. "Something like that awful machete Santiago wears on his belt!"

"Machete?" repeated someone from behind them. The voice had the salty rasp of a veteran sailor. Sun-bleached hair, a week's worth of stubble, and a checkered shirt over torn jeans completed the picture. He wiped the grease and oil from his hands. "I heard that. What about Santiago's machete?"

Agatha recognized the man from his photo on the EyeNet. It was Davey O'Connor, the *Loki's* Irish steward.

"Now, Miss, has this beautiful white cat got your tongue?" he chuckled, slipping a chipped wooden pipe into the corner of his mouth.

"No, Mr. O'Connor, my tongue is right where it belongs," replied Agatha. "And something's not right on this boat!" She explained the reason for their visit for the umpteenth time. "So we need to hear your version of events and check the cargo hold," she concluded.

Davey O'Connor pulled a flask from the back pocket of his jeans. "First I'll take a sip of my medicine, if you don't mind." A moment later, they were walking along the narrow corridor in the bowels of the ship, approaching the hold.

The air smelled briny and stale. O'Connor sat on an old crate and began to speak.

"The other night, I came down here to secure the cargo while the storm was raging. I've never seen anything like that storm, let me tell you!" He stared at the floorboards for a moment. "Then we must've hit a rock, because we started taking on water. That's the last thing you want, especially in a storm."

"Were you by yourself?" asked Agatha.

"I had my pipe," said the Irishman, smiling. He cleared his throat, took another sip from his flask, and continued his story. "Since I couldn't stop up the leak on my own, I called for the captain."

"How did you contact the captain?" Agatha interrupted.

"As I was rushing up to get him, I ran into Ramona. She's a lovely lass, isn't she? She offered to go fetch the captain, so I came back down here and got to work while I waited for Larsson to come lend a hand."

"Are you positive it was Ramona?" asked Dash.

"Well, that's what she told me," replied the Irishman. "I swear, I can never tell those two apart. They are every bit as pretty as each other, don't you think?"

Uncle Conrad gave him a smile of agreement.

"What happened after the captain arrived?" Agatha continued.

"We played checkers!" he said, then burst out laughing. "What else do you do when the ship's got a leak?" Agatha looked baffled. "Excuse the joke, Miss. Where was I? Oh yes, Larsson came rushing below and we got to work on the pumps because the hold was flooding."

"How long did he stay down here?"

The Irishman took another sip. "Must have been close to an hour or so," he said vaguely. "Takes a lot of elbow grease to pump out a hold, you know? When I saw that I could handle the rest by myself, I told the captain to go back up to the bridge. A few minutes later, I found out the

golden calendar had gone overboard. Larsson knows some very colorful curses, and his voice travels a long way!" he concluded with a chuckle.

Chandler carefully observed the hull. "I suppose the leak has been repaired?" he said.

"It surely has, my friend," replied O'Connor, pointing to the starboard. "There's where it was. I finished welding a patch on it this morning."

The Hole in the Hull

Agatha headed over to inspect it. Dash and Uncle Conrad followed, while Chandler stayed behind, listening politely while the Irishman rambled on about the miraculous properties of the medicine in his flask.

At the bottom of the hold, the repair was easy to spot. There was a copper patch and a blackened smear left by a blowtorch.

Uncle Conrad knelt down and ran his hand over the patch. "Hmmm . . ," he muttered.

"What is it?" asked Dash softly.

"I could be wrong, but this repair . . . well, it doesn't seem recent to me."

"What makes you think that?" Agatha asked in a whisper.

"That solder looks fresh enough, but the patch is already beginning to oxidize. That's a sign of a much older repair," he explained.

"Are you sure?"

"No doubt in my mind," he said. "I've been

knocking around on boats for years, and I've seen a lot of hull patches."

"So, Miss, are you satisfied?" interrupted the Irishman, shaking his flask.

"Indeed," replied Agatha. "Thanks for your time."

"It's nothing. I'm always pleased to assist a lovely young lass such as yourself. Come and find me again soon. It gets mighty lonely down here."

Agatha led the group back up into the sunlight.

"Well, what do you think?" asked Dash dubiously.

The young girl stroked her turned-up nose. "O'Connor's story confirms the captain's alibi— at least that he was down in the hold. But that repair is a fake, according to Uncle Conrad. I suspect the steward is hiding something, too. Maybe they're in cahoots."

"It's nearly evening," said Dash, sounding

The Hole in the Hull

worried. "I have a bad feeling that we'll never get to the bottom of this!"

"Don't worry," Agatha soothed him. "We still need to interview Richie Stark. Maybe he'll be able to shed some light on the situation!"

$\mathcal{A}$s they made their way to the opposite end of the *Loki*, Chandler raised a question that left them all deep in thought. "Do you still believe Captain Larsson is responsible for the calendar's disappearance?" he asked.

"At this point in the investigation, the only thing that we have against him is McBain's suspicion," said Agatha. "On the other hand, we've collected evidence that raises questions about everyone else on the crew."

"You're in a very difficult line of work, kids," Uncle Conrad grinned. "I'd rather hang out with the dolphins and ride on a Jet Ski!"

"The solution will fall into place eventually, you'll see," Agatha assured him. "It always works like that, doesn't it, Dash?"

The young detective snapped his fingers. "That's it!" he cried. "Maybe Captain Larsson left false clues all over the ship, and we've fallen for them, hook, line, and sinker!"

Agatha let out a hearty laugh. "Dear cousin, the most likely explanation is usually the simplest," she said. "I don't think the captain would have had time to lay down a whole trail of false clues. Plus, even though Larsson didn't know it, Richie Stark works for McBain, and he's been keeping an eye on Captain Larsson this whole time. If the captain got caught leaving false clues, McBain would probably already know about it!"

The chugging of the ship's engine was overrun by the deafening sound of heavy-metal music. Thrashing guitars and a tuneless voice

wailed from the doorway of the ship's laboratory. Peering through the porthole-shaped window in the door, Agatha saw a sloppily dressed young man hunched over a desktop computer. He had his back to the door, and didn't realize that he was being watched.

"Hey, Agatha! Look at the screen!" exclaimed Dash.

The monitor showed a detailed relief map of the Florida coastline, with a flashing red light that seemed to be moving somewhere out in the ocean.

"Looks like a satellite-recovery program,"

The Floating Lab

murmured Agatha. Her expression hardened. "It's about time we solved this mystery. I suggest we don't let Richie know we've been spying on him."

Chandler knocked so hard that Richie Stark shot up out of his chair. "Whoa! What was that, an earthquake?" he cried, turning toward the door. His pale complexion was offset by his black T-shirt, and despite his annoyed expression, he had a baby face. According to the file, he was twenty-five years old, but he looked even younger.

"Mr. McBain sent us," explained Agatha as they entered the lab. "We'd like to have a chat with you."

"Yeah, sure." Richie Stark hurriedly turned off the computer and lowered the volume of his blasting music. He looked nervous.

The lab was crammed wall-to-wall with computers and marine-research instruments: navigational systems, deep-sea thermometers, hydrological scanners, Fathometers, sonars, ocean-floor mapping devices, drills, and a thousand other electronic gadgets.

Dash raised the patch from his eye and looked around, awestruck.

Agatha had already begun questioning the technician. "Mr. McBain told us you've been working for him, is that right?"

"You got it," said Richie, with a bit of a stammer. "I supervise all the research and analyze the data."

"And keep a close eye on the captain, too," Dash added.

The technician's pale face pinkened. "Umm . . . let's just say that Mr. McBain was very convincing when he offered to double my pay . . . ," he admitted sheepishly.

"We don't have a problem with that," Agatha cut him off. "What we want to know is if you have any conclusive proof that the captain is responsible for this theft."

Richie shook his head. "I wish. But I can't prove a thing," he replied. "Larsson is a pretty sly dog. For some time now, he's been lobbying hard to replace this old tub with a brand-new ship. That costs lots of money."

"That's it?" asked Dash. "That's what you've based your suspicions on, that he wants a new boat?"

Richie looked cornered. "He knows every

corner of the *Loki*. He could have hidden the calendar anywhere!"

"To be honest," Chandler interrupted politely, "I don't see how he could have managed that by himself. A yard's worth of gold would weigh—"

"Yes! That's exactly my point!" cried the young man, jumping to his feet. "The captain is a man of many resources, and he must have had an accomplice!"

"Like a young lab technician, for instance?" Agatha suggested with a smile.

"Where were you during the storm?" Dash asked.

"Right here in the lab," Richie responded. "I could see from my weather data that the storm was gonna be bad, and I wanted to back up the rest of the research data in case we lost power."

"Did you see anything unusual?"

"Not a thing. I stayed in the lab the whole time, getting seasick as we got tossed around by

the waves. Then the captain rushed in to tell me that the calendar was missing, and I spent the rest of the night on the bridge, repairing the radar and echo sounder so we could start searching for it in the morning."

"Larsson told us that there was a lot of damage, and that the AUV sank," Agatha said.

"The Shark just about had a stroke when I told him the AUV was gone," said Richie. "That thing cost him millions of dollars!"

Uncle Conrad gave a whistle. "It's that expensive?"

"It was a next-generation prototype . . ."

"Can you tell us about it, Richie?" asked Agatha.

The man's eyes lit up, and he immediately became more enthusiastic about talking to the group. Clearly research was his passion, and talking about it electrified him. "Well, you see, normally an AUV has very specific instruments:

sonar for identifying submerged objects, a magnetometer for detecting metal objects, a current meter for measuring marine flow, and lots of other analytical apparatuses," he rattled off.

"Do you control it from inside the lab?" asked Dash.

"Not exactly. The AUV is a type of robot. I enter the research coordinates, and it maneuvers itself. My job is to analyze the data and refine its movements by entering new coordinates."

Agatha stopped scribbling in her notebook and interrupted him. "What additional instruments did this next-generation prototype have?"

"It was equipped with two mechanical arms for working on the seabed, and a set of solar panels to increase its range," replied the

technician. "But the most useful thing for our purposes was a powerful claw for picking up objects, even when they're buried beneath sand and debris. That's what enabled us to recover the calendar. In fact, I can show you how it works."

He turned on his computer, clicking open a video file. "Look, the AUV's cameras captured the whole salvage operation. See how the claw is lifting it up?"

They all turned their attention to the screen.

Richie continued enthusiastically. "If you're into this stuff, I have thousands of photos of the seabed, the wreck, and a lot of weird deepwater fish," he added. "It's a whole different planet down there!"

Agatha gently nudged Dash with her elbow, whispering something into his ear.

"Hey, Richie, could you burn me a copy of this material?" asked the young detective, pulling out his EyeNet. "Mr. McBain will be thrilled if we come back with some evidence."

"Sure thing. Got a flash drive?"

Dash pushed a sequence of buttons, then handed over his EyeNet.

Richie's eyes lit up at the sight of an unfamiliar electronic toy. "Hey, what is this thing?" he asked.

"A new portable media player," Dash lied.

"Cool! As soon as we get back on land, I'm gonna order one!"

Richie connected the EyeNet via the USB port and started uploading his files. The transfer was completed within a couple of minutes.

"Do you have any more questions? I love meeting new people, especially fellow tech geeks," said the young technician, grinning at Dash. "All I've seen for the past few months are the ugly mugs of the captain and crew!"

"They're not *all* ugly mugs," said Uncle Conrad.

The Floating Lab

Richie laughed. "Yeah, right! Those Sanchez twins are something else. Did you see——"

"Thanks," Agatha interrupted. "That's all we need for now."

Richie said good-bye and turned back to his computer.

Back on the *Loki*'s deck, Agatha found a place away from prying eyes and turned to Dash. "So, what did you get?"

Chandler rubbed his forehead. "Did I miss something?"

"Agatha suggested that I should use the Argonaut," Dash explained. "It's a sophisticated kind of computer virus that instantly sifts through data on a computer. Since it was developed using a new programming language, no other software can detect it."

"You're just full of surprises, young nephew," said Conrad Mistery enthusiastically, slapping him on the shoulder once again.

The results from their scheme were amazing.

"The Argonaut reconstructed a file that was double-deleted yesterday," exclaimed Dash as he read the display. "It is coordinates for a route starting right here on the *Loki* and ending in . . . Miami, Florida!"

"It must have been for the AUV," said Agatha. "That means Captain Larsson wasn't the one who stole the calendar!"

The others stared at her, stunned.

"It was Richie Stark?" asked Chandler.

Agatha stroked the tip of her nose. "The mystery is solved, colleagues!" she announced. "But to unmask the culprit, I'll need Uncle Conrad to do me a small favor . . ."

CHAPTER EIGHT

A Well-Considered Plan

Following his brilliant niece's orders, Conrad Mistery invited Captain Larsson for dinner on his yacht. The burly Norwegian was a little resistant, but the idea of eating something tastier than the slop that O'Connor usually dished out convinced him to accept. The sound of clinking plates and glasses, and Larsson's coarse voice singing sea chanteys, sounded from Conrad's boat.

Meanwhile, Agatha gathered the rest of the crew on the deck.

Chandler stood beside the young mistress with his big arms folded, while Dash nervously rubbed his temples, and Watson continued to prowl the deck, sniffing for traces of fish. The sky had clouded over and only the glow of the boat's running lights illuminated the *Loki*.

"Friends, I'm about to explain what happened on the night the calendar disappeared," Agatha began calmly.

"Awesome!" exclaimed Ramira happily. "Just like a TV mystery!"

"Couldn't we have done this below deck?" grumbled O'Connor. "My bones are too old to be standing outside on a damp night."

A Well-Considered Plan

Santiago didn't say anything. He simply stared at them with narrowed eyes.

"The calendar was positioned right where we're standing now," Agatha continued, pointing to the deck. "According to the captain's theory, the Mayan disk was thrown overboard during the storm. But that isn't what happened."

No one said a word.

Agatha moved toward the bow, followed by the rest of the group. "The most curious thing about this case was the abundance of clues. Of course, none of them are definitive, and nothing points directly at Captain Larsson . . ."

"That doesn't mean he's not the culprit," Richie objected.

Agatha stopped next to the pulley Santiago had finished repairing. "Over to you, cousin," she said.

Dash reached between the crates and pulled out the severed metal cable Chandler had found that afternoon.

"As you can see, it was cut clean through. To do so would require a very sharp weapon, like Santiago's machete."

"What are you trying to say, little boy?" growled the hulking boatswain.

"Señor Santiago, I am simply saying that you lied when you told us that the cable broke during the storm," replied Dash.

"After we found this clue," Agatha continued, "we interviewed the Sanchez sisters. There were several contradictions in their account of what happened that night—for example, which sister had let Larsson know there was a leak in the hold."

"So the captain made a mistake!" protested Ramona. "That's not our fault!"

"Maybe not," said Agatha, smiling. "Larsson also said that he saw you both wearing wet raincoats, but you said you spent the storm inside your cabin, working on your diving gear."

A Well-Considered Plan

"So that means the captain lied twice!" interrupted Ramira. She sounded angry.

"Everyone knows he's a liar!" Ramona agreed.

"Maybe he is, but not about this," responded Agatha. "Anyway, let's move on. Mr. O'Connor, would you be so kind as to escort us down to the hold?"

The Irishman led the way, guided by the galley lights. He cast a furtive glance at the patched-up hole.

Agatha noticed, but didn't comment. "Mr. O'Connor told us that the boat was taking on water and that he had asked for the captain's help," she recounted.

"That's right, I surely did," O'Connor agreed.

"It's too bad that this hole wasn't caused by the storm. The repair is too old. So the only logical conclusion is that you must have been trying to lure the captain away from the bridge. Could you tell us why?"

The Irishman held his tongue, taking an extra-long sip of his medicine.

"Never mind, I'll tell you why," announced Agatha. "The purpose of Mr. O'Connor's staged flood was to keep the captain distracted by work for 'an hour or so'—the time needed to make the precious Mayan calendar disappear!"

The silence following this statement seemed to go on forever.

Agatha continued. "Now let's proceed to the lab," she said calmly. "Richie, could you please lead the way?"

A few minutes later, they stood in front of the bank of computer equipment.

"When we paid Richie a visit here this afternoon, we found out something interesting. Isn't that right, Dash?" Agatha started.

"Exactly!" her cousin said, joining her at center stage. "We found that the AUV never actually sank, because right at this very

A Well-Considered Plan

moment, it's heading to Florida!"

The young technician paled.

"According to the current coordinates," Dash continued, tapping the screen of his EyeNet, "it seems to be heading toward the Miami Maritime Museum."

"I don't know where they're getting these crazy theories from," blurted Ramona.

"We're trying to figure out who stole the calendar," Agatha replied with a clever smile.

"Actually, we already know who it was, but poor Richie is going to pay the price for the rest of the team."

"Me? But, why me?" whispered Richie in desperation.

"Because you're the one who reprogrammed the AUV," explained Dash. "I'm sure the Miami police will want to have a chat with you when they find the calendar on board."

Richie gazed around in bewilderment. He

seemed about to blurt out something, but he kept his mouth shut.

"Do you really have nothing to add?" Agatha asked the crew. "If so, then it's up to me to reconstruct the full story. The whole theft was planned in advance, and the storm provided the perfect cover," she said. "While the captain was busy in the hold with O'Connor, the rest of you helped transport the gold disk to the AUV. It was a tricky job because the weather made moving around very difficult: the wind, the waves, the tilting of the boat. Also, the relic is huge and extremely heavy."

"But the AUV wouldn't have enough space for an object that size, you little busybody," Ramira protested.

"Explain that if you can," snapped Ramona.

"Richie provided me with that answer, as well," said Agatha.

"M-m-me?" stammered Richie.

A Well-Considered Plan

"Yes, that's right. The calendar was attached to the AUV's claw—the one you explained had been added to the new prototype. You entered new coordinates into the navigation system, Santiago cut the cable, and then you went around the ship causing more damage so the captain wouldn't be suspicious that only the calendar and the AUV robot went missing. Then you tried

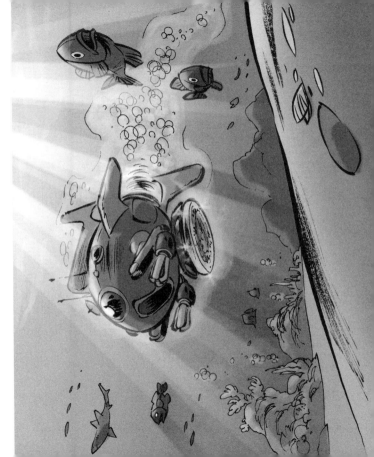

to blame the whole thing on the storm." Agatha paused briefly, then turned to the twins. "When the captain came back to look for Santiago, he spotted you in your wet raincoats. You'd just come back down from the deck and hadn't had time to take them off yet—isn't that right?"

"You can't prove a thing, little girl," Santiago said slowly.

"No, I can't," Agatha admitted. "It's still unclear to me *why* you plotted to steal the calendar. I suspect it wasn't because it is worth so much money. The AUV is heading straight for the Miami Maritime Museum, which makes me suspect . . ."

Dash and Chandler exchanged nervous glances. Agatha was now at the most crucial juncture.

"Fine, we'll explain the whole thing," sighed O'Connor. "It's not right that poor Richie should take all the blame." He gave the

---

technician a pat on the back. "Go on, son, explain everything."

The technician cleared his throat. "I'd been listening in on a phone conversation between McBain and Captain Larsson," he whispered. "The Shark told the captain that the location of the *Alcazar* had been revealed to the curator at the museum, who wanted to put it on public display. Having extorted the information he needed, McBain decided to recover the calendar for himself before the museum could get to it."

"When Richie told us what was going on, my sister and I decided to get involved," Ramona interrupted. "Since we're from Mexico and the Mayans were our ancestors, we wanted the calendar to end up in a museum, where it could show the world our people's great artistic achievements."

"And you, Señor Santiago?" asked Agatha.

The Cuban man snorted. "We need to respect

all beliefs. The Mayan calendar belongs to the gods. It's not right that greedy men like McBain and the captain should profit from it. Yemaya would praise me for helping the boy!"

Agatha turned to O'Connor, who sighed.

"I only got involved because I can't stand Captain Larsson. He's a good-for-nothing liar who wouldn't hesitate to commit a crime for money. He's always treated me like trash. Well, now he can't afford to buy the shiny new boat he's been craving. That was reason enough for me, Miss."

"So you can't just blame Richie," Ramira declared. "We were all in this together."

"Will you turn us in?" Richie asked in dismay.

"Will you tell McBain the whole story?"

Agatha picked up Watson. "I'm not happy about working for Mr. McBain myself," she admitted. "But this is my cousin's case, so it's up to him to decide what the right thing to do is."

CHAPTER EIGHT

A Well-Considered Plan

Dash looked at the Cuban man, who was so proud of his beliefs; the twins, who just wanted to stand up for their people; the old steward, who was weary from years of oppression; and Richie, a fellow tech geek, not much older than himself, who was full of ideals. He let out a long sigh, then made his decision. "Even the best detectives lose a case every once in a while," he reassured them with a hint of a smile.

Mystery Solved...

Back at Uncle Conrad's water park, they phoned McBain to tell him they'd been unable to find evidence that the Mayan calendar had been stolen by anyone. The billionaire was furious, and told them he'd be complaining to the upper echelon of Eye International about the incompetence of its agents.

Dash spent long hours tossing sleeplessly in his bed. This case would be his first failure, but he still felt proud of having supported the crew's plan to hijack the calendar from McBain. In some ways, he, too, was an accomplice in the theft, but he decided there was some honor to

be had in robbing a shark.

He fell asleep with this thought just as dawn started to break. But all too soon, he was abruptly awakened.

"Come on, you slug!" roared Uncle Conrad, throwing the windows wide open. "It's a gorgeous day in Bermuda! Let's send you back home with a tan!"

Blinding sunlight hit the young detective, and he hid his head under the pillow. His uncle reached over and pulled it away, laughing. "Everyone's waiting for you!" He beamed. "Jet Ski safari!"

These were exactly the magic words that Dash needed to hear.

He jumped out of bed and went down to the patio to gorge himself on guavas, papayas, and pineapple. He could see Agatha and Chandler swimming around in the pool with the dolphins. Watson had climbed up onto the trampoline and

was looking down at Agatha and Chandler with suspicion, as if he was afraid they'd switched species.

Dash felt a hearty thump on his back. "Put on this life jacket, Dash," said Uncle Conrad in a hearty voice. "I wouldn't want to have to call the lifeguard because you've fallen into the lagoon!"

They walked down to a small turquoise bay overlooking the ocean. The water was so clear

Mystery Solved . . .

that they could see tropical fish swimming in the coral reef half a mile away.

"Good morning, Dash!" Agatha greeted him with a smile. She was already perched on a sparkling silver Jet Ski.

"Did you sleep well?" Chandler asked him. His Jet Ski was black and wobbled under his extreme weight.

Dash gave them a confident grin. "As soon as

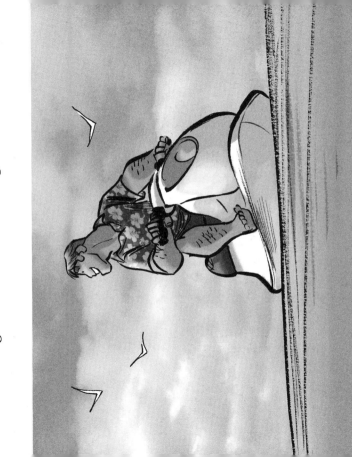

Uncle Conrad gives us the signal, I'm going to be flying across the water!" he declared, boarding a flame-red model.

"Everyone ready to go?" asked Conrad Mistery, turning toward them. "I call this a Jet Ski safari because we're off to explore otherwise inaccessible areas. Needless to say, they are incredibly beautiful!"

"So what are we waiting for?" Dash asked, challenging him. "I've ridden these beauties before. I'm a Jet Ski rock star!" He turned on the engine, pushed the START button, and took off like a rocket.

Behind him, his uncle shouted, "Dash, be careful! It's not a race!"

The young detective laughed and stood up on his toes to go even faster. He wanted to get out to the middle of the lagoon, where he could show off his acrobatic maneuvers. But after a few moments of feeling the rush, his waterproof

Mystery Solved . . .

titanium device vibrated in the pocket of his surf shorts. He slowed right down, pulled out the EyeNet, and saw a message from his school on the screen.

"Uh-oh, what now?" he muttered, hesitating. He turned red as a lobster as he contemplated the failure notification the message was sure to contain.

The others caught up to him and saw him staring at his EyeNet.

"This is going to be hard on him," Agatha whispered to Chandler. "Who knows what nasty things McBain told his teachers about our 'failed' mission."

Uncle Conrad dived right in. "What's got you looking so spooked, Dash?" he barked, scaring away every fish within yards. "Man up and face your fears! Get it over with, boy!"

Dash shook himself and stared at his companions in terror. "Do I really have to open

this message?" he asked in a barely audible voice.

They all nodded.

"Okay, here goes nothing. If I have been expelled from school, at least it was for a good cause!"

He pushed a button and stared at the screen.

As he scrolled through the message, a smile lit up his face. "I've been promoted!" he shouted. "The museum's curator safely received the Mayan calendar and sent his congratulations to all of us!"

Agatha moved her Jet Ski over closer to Dash's. She scanned the message quickly and immediately understood what had happened.

"They were testing you, Dash!" she said, grinning. "They knew how greedy McBain was and wanted to find out how you would handle a client like that!"

The two children hugged one another, while Uncle Conrad and Chandler traded proud glances.

Mystery Solved . . .

"Brilliant!" said their uncle with an enormous smile. "Now, what do you say we keep going with our safari? If we head out to those sandbars over there, we'll be able to see the remains of an old shipwreck . . ."

He didn't even have time to finish his whole sentence before Dash took off, even faster than before. "I'm the best detective in the world!" he screamed at the top of his lungs, ecstatic.

Unfortunately, there was a big flat rock just under the surface. Dash didn't see it and kept accelerating. His Jet Ski started to swerve, then bounced up into the air as if it were jumping off a trampoline.

"HELLLLPP!" Dash's shout echoed across the lagoon as the world's best detective did a triple somersault, diving face-first into the crystal-clear waters of the Bermuda Triangle.

Agatha

Girl of Mystery

Agatha's Next Mystery:
The Crown of Venice

The Investigation Begins . . .

It was a Sunday morning in the middle of February when a loud blare of trumpets rattled the window glass of the penthouse apartment above Baker Palace. The stereo's surround sound was state of the art; it sounded as if General Custer himself had come back to life and ordered his bugler to play right into the ear of the tall teenage boy stretched out on the sofa.

Dashiell Mistery jolted awake, as quickly as if someone had thrown him under an ice-cold shower. His hair flopped over his forehead as he clapped his hands over his ears and jumped into action, dodging piles of clothes and stray electronic devices to slam down the volume control on his stereo. The trumpets cut off midnote.

Dash stood panting with relief, his eyes puffy from lack of sleep. It was eight in the morning. His brand-new alarm system had done the trick, but the fourteen-year-old student at Eye International Detective Academy couldn't remember why in the world he had set it to go off so early. He scratched his head as memories of the previous night began to seep through the fog around his brain. "Oh no," he groaned in despair. "My Criminal Physiognomy class! I better get to work!"

In a flash, he was sprawled in his swivel chair, staring at his army of computers. Every one of the monitor screens was open to *Alien Hunt,* an online video game in which a squad of action heroes patrols a space station, wiping out monsters from outer space.

He'd spent most of the week in the avatar of Phil Destroy, a cyborg warrior armed to the teeth. In a week of marathon sessions, Dash had worked his way up to the national finals, taking on top-ranked players with names like Killderella and Exterminizer. Meanwhile, he'd completely neglected his Criminal Physiognomy homework, and now he was terrified that Professor FB32, who had a sixth sense for sniffing out slackers, would pick on him to answer questions in the class's next videoconference.

Would he make a fool of himself? In just a few minutes, his teacher's face would appear on the screen. He had to get ready immediately!

Feeling frantic, Dash logged off *Alien Hunt* and picked up the printouts and notes strewn all over his desk. He formed a mound of paper in front of him, picked up a yellow highlighter, and started to cram. Physiognomy was a difficult subject—it involved looking for clues about a person from their appearance, especially facial features.

"Okay, okay . . . what does it mean when the subject has a unibrow?" Dash muttered to himself. He searched through his notes until he found a scrawl on the back of a candy wrapper. "Ah, here we go," he went on. "It's a clear sign of an inclination toward theft!"

He narrowed his eyes and continued to work his way down the review questions. "Who came up with this theory?" he read.

Dash didn't need to dig through his notes for the answer to this question. "Simple!" he crowed. "Cesare Lombroso! His theory was later debunked by two other professors . . . wait, what were their names again?" He rifled through his pile of paper.

"Where are my historical notes?" he cried in desperation. He remembered that Cesare Lombroso's nineteenth-century theories had been revised from top to bottom. But who had done it, and why?

"I don't have a clue," he groaned. "I really need to pay more attention and take better notes! Now what will I tell the professor?"

To make matters worse, the Eye International symbol suddenly flashed on the screen of his main computer, followed by a message:

CONNECTING, PLEASE WAIT.

Dash ran his hands through his hair. "I'm sunk!" he repeated again and again.

But weirdly, the face that appeared on his screen was not his professor but the school secretary, a middle-aged woman with frown lines framing her mouth. "We're sorry to inform you that Agent FB32 is engaged in a mission and won't be able to teach today's class," she announced. "The Criminal Physiognomy class is postponed until next Sunday. Happy investigating, everyone!"

The smile on Dash's face spread from one ear to the other. What amazing luck! Now he had a whole week to revisit the topic and take better notes, and he decided to start right away. But his stomach was growling. It wouldn't hurt to have something for breakfast first, would it? He picked up the phone and ordered his favorite breakfast: a three-cheese pizza with double pepperoni, anchovies, and jalapeños. He'd nicknamed it "Zombie Pizza" because the smell alone could wake the dead.

He had just put down the phone when a *BLIP!* let him know that his friends were online for a game of *Alien Hunt.*

"I can't give in to temptation," Dash lectured himself. "I have to focus on my detective career."

But his resistance crumbled in seconds. "I've got a whole week," he told himself. He swiveled to face his gaming computer, put on his headset, and greeted Clarke and Mallory, whose avatars were waiting for him at the entrance to the first level. Phil Destroy entered the dark corridors of the spaceship, overcome with the thrill of the challenge.

"Blast that monster! Zap it!" Clarke's voice shouted through the headphones.

"Look out! They're coming out of the walls!" Mallory yelled at the top of her lungs.

"I'll have to bounce pretty soon, guys," Dash interrupted. "I'm getting a pizza delivered."

"Hey, Dash, did you hear about all the apartment thefts?" asked Clarke.

"No, what happened?"

"Scotland Yard says every one of the victims had a pizza delivered right before they noticed their stuff had gone missing," his friend explained.

"It happened to us," added Mallory. "They stole my mom's silver teapot."

Dash snickered. If the police had called him

to investigate, he would have solved the case by now.

"They wouldn't have much luck with me," he declared between blasts of his turbocharged ray gun. "I'm much too smart to fall for a scam like that!"

The ring of the doorbell distracted Dash from the game. He swung the door open and welcomed the pizza-delivery man. His name was Derek; he was a nice guy who always told Dash wild stories about his deliveries around the city. And he didn't have a unibrow, so he was clearly not a thief!

"That's sixteen bucks," said Derek.

After digging around on the table, Dash managed to unearth his wallet and hand over a twenty. Derek walked off, thanking him for the generous tip.

But the morning still had surprises in store. As he scarfed down his first slice of hot Zombie

Pizza, the aspiring detective noticed that the special titanium device hanging on its hook above the sofa was flashing.

"Dash! What are you doing? We're getting annihilated!" Clarke's protests rang over the headphones.

Dash ignored him and grabbed his titanium EyeNet, the high-tech device used by every student at his detective school. The message on the screen made him immediately lose his appetite.

INVESTIGATION IN VENICE! UTMOST URGENCY. CONSULT THE ATTACHED FILES ASAP.

Dash abandoned his half-eaten pizza and took off like an intercontinental missile to his cousin Agatha's. He left the apartment so fast that he didn't even notice his favorite baseball glove had vanished.